Grand Canyon Village

Bright Angel Trailhead

Indian Garden

Devil's Corkscrew

Plateau Point

River Trail

The
GRAND
CANYON

Liz Garton Scanlon

In the
CANYON

illustrated by

Ashley Wolff

Beach Lane Books
New York   London   Toronto   Sydney   New Delhi

For Marla.—L. G. S.

For Martin Litton, who listened
to his own control tower. Thank you.—A. W.

BEACH LANE BOOKS

An imprint of Simon & Schuster Children's Publishing Division · 1230 Avenue of
the Americas, New York, New York 10020 · Text copyright © 2015 by Elizabeth
Garton Scanlon · Illustrations copyright © 2015 by Ashley Wolff · All rights
reserved, including the right of reproduction in whole or in part in any form. ·
BEACH LANE BOOKS is a trademark of Simon & Schuster, Inc. · For information
about special discounts for bulk purchases, please contact Simon & Schuster Special
Sales at 1-866-506-1949 or business@simonandschuster.com. · The Simon & Schuster
Speakers Bureau can bring authors to your live event. For more information or to book an
event, contact the Simon & Schuster Speakers Bureau at 1-866-248-3049 or visit our website
at www.simonspeakers.com. · Book design by Lauren Rille · The text for this book is set in
Bodoni Egyptian. · The illustrations for this book are rendered using linoleum block prints,
printed in black ink, colored with gouache, on Arches Cover paper. · Manufactured in China
· 0615 SCP · First Edition · 10 9 8 7 6 5 4 3 2 1 · Library of Congress Cataloging-
in-Publication Data · Scanlon, Elizabeth Garton. · In the canyon / Liz Garton Scanlon ;
Illustrated by Ashley Wolff.—First edition. · p. cm. · Summary: Illustrations and simple rhyming
text present a child who is hiking with a group into the Grand Canyon, enjoying the wonders of
nature—whether a lizard, a picture on the stone, or a glimpse of the moon from the bottom. · ISBN
978-1-4814-0348-1 (hardcover) · ISBN 978-1-4814-0349-8 (eBook) · [1. Stories in rhyme. 2. Grand
Canyon (Ariz.)—Fiction. 3. Nature—Fiction. 4. Hiking—Fiction.] I. Wolff, Ashley, illustrator. II. Title. ·
PZ8.3.S2798In 2015 · [E]—dc23 · 2014008254

Here's a map, some boots, a pack,
a walking stick, and sandy track.

Here's the ranger, badge and brim,
and here's a camp jay, watching him.

Here's a footstep, dusty red,
another one, and more ahead—

down this twisty, weavy way,
through golden yellow, green, and gray.

Here's a little hidey-hole,
home to sneaky squirrel or vole.

Hello, pictures in the stone,
living out here so alone—

do you watch the mules in line
brushing past the cactus spines?

Now here's a tiny slice of shade,
a yummy lunch, some lemonade,

and a lizard, still as sand,
his head all speckled, body tan.

Moving on, so hot, so slow,
a condor shows which way to go.

TRAIL →

Here's a tree with roots in rock,
and hello, Mr. Red-Tailed Hawk!

The clouds come up, the wind blows in,
the shadows fall upon hot skin.

Now it's really getting steep,
and there's the river, way down deep!

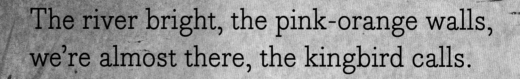

The river bright, the pink-orange walls,
we're almost there, the kingbird calls.

We reach the bottom, look back up.
We've dropped into a rocky cup!

Here's the dark, and here's the shine,
and here's the moon—it's like it's mine!—
to tuck inside me, way down deep . . .

grand and wild,
mine to keep.

Author's Note

I was in my early twenties when a friend and I hiked from the rim of the Grand Canyon all the way down to the Colorado River and back. It was a hot, hard adventure. Some folks wore bandannas over their mouths to keep from breathing in the kicked-up dust. And we saw one young guy turn his jeans into cut-off shorts with a pocketknife, just to keep cool! But the staggering size and beauty of the place made the sweat, dirt, and blisters worth it. The Grand Canyon—a 277-mile-long channel through northern Arizona—is over a mile deep in some places, and the walls reveal rock that is nearly two billion years old. It's home to plentiful wildlife, a wide array of rock-loving plants, and many ancient petroglyphs, not to mention a ridiculously exquisite sunrise and sunset each and every day. In a word, it's grand! But to me, the most astonishing thing about hiking there was that instead of feeling dwarfed by the grandeur, I felt embraced by it. I felt like it showed me its many miraculous secrets. I think this is something we all want and need—to become one with our wild places, so that even when we're not in the wilderness, it is forever inside of us. That's what I imagine for the little girl in this book, and for her parents, and for you, too.

Glossary

Cactus: Cacti are desert-loving plants that have sharp spines instead of leaves and a waxy coating that helps them retain water. There are many kinds of cacti in the Grand Canyon, including ones with funny names like fishhook, hedgehog, beavertail, and desert prickly pear.

Camp jay: "Camp jay" or "camp robber" are really just nicknames for different species of jays that live in and around the canyon. These include the pinyon jay and the Steller's jay, birds that eat seeds, fruit, and insects—but also steal pretzels and bread crusts from unsuspecting hikers and campers!

Condor: California condors were nearly extinct until conservationists began to breed them in captivity and then reintroduce them to wild places, including the Grand Canyon. Many of them wear numbered tags so the conservationists can observe their success. Condors are huge vultures—their wings can stretch up to 9 ½ feet wide! They roost on the cliffs and in tall trees. Lucky visitors see them there or soaring on the thermals overhead as they search for food.

Kingbird: A few different varieties of kingbirds make their home in the canyon. All have gray feathers and white markings on their tails; Western and Cassin's kingbirds have yellow bellies too. These songbirds aren't large, but they are bossy and protective of their territory. They'll use their sharp songs to stand up to crows, red-tailed hawks, and other big birds.

Mules: Mules are a cross between a horse and a donkey. They are sure-footed, hardy, and smart, which makes them well suited for canyon life. Some visitors take short rides along the rim and others take overnight trips—all the way down to the river. It's easier than hiking, but most people end up with sore bottoms from all that time in a saddle!

Pictures in the stone: The best evidence we have that ancient people lived in the canyon comes from the petroglyphs or rock art on the canyon walls. Early artists made petroglyphs by chipping away flakes of red rock with stone tools, exposing pale designs and figures that can still be seen today.

Pink-orange walls: Sandstone and shale are just two of the many kinds of rock visible in the Grand Canyon. Over billions of years, layers of sand and ash settled, tectonic plates shifted and collided, volcanic magma rose and cooled, and rocks were eroded by the Colorado River, leaving the many colorful layers of the canyon we see today.

Ranger: Rangers are the professionals tasked with protecting and preserving our nation's many parks. They also help keep visitors safe and informed. All National Park Service Rangers wear a familiar uniform, badge, and hat so they're easy to find if you have questions or need help.

Red-tailed hawk: Red-tailed hawks glide and dive like eagles, but they're much smaller. They can be identified by their white bellies and their red tails. Red-tailed hawks have plentiful prey in the canyon, including rattlesnakes. Sometimes they'll catch a snake and then drop it from an extreme height to make sure it's dead before eating it!

River: The Colorado River isn't just at the bottom of the canyon—it *created* the canyon! Millions of years ago, the river charted a course through the massive Colorado Plateau and began its work of powerful erosion. The 1,450-mile river runs from the Rocky Mountains all the way to the Gulf of California; 277 of those miles are through the canyon.

There is abundant wildlife living in and around the Grand Canyon, thanks to the diverse and protected habitats in the park. Visitors might spot any of the hundreds of species of mammals, birds, reptiles, fish, and amphibians, including the ones listed above, as well as bald eagles, mountain lions, bighorn sheep, mule deer, lizards, and snakes.

For further Grand Canyon reading and exploration, visit:

The National Park Service: nps.gov/grca and nps.gov/grca/forkids

The Grand Canyon Association: grandcanyon.org

National Geographic:

travel.nationalgeographic.com/travel/national-parks/grand-canyon-national-park